HOT FUDGE PICKLES

Published by Willowisp Press, Inc.
401 E. Wilson Bridge Road, Worthington, Ohio 43085

Copyright ©1984 by Willowisp Press, Inc.

All rights reserved. No portion of this book may be reproduced, stored in a retrieval system, or transmitted, in any form or by any means, electronic, mechanical, photocopying, recording, or otherwise without prior written permission from the publisher.

Printed in the United States of America

10 9 8 7 6 5 4 3

ISBN 0-87406-216-0

HOT FUDGE PICKLES

by Marilyn D. Anderson

illustrated by Tammy Starner-Altop

Chapter 1

I'll never know what made Alvin Jones do it. I'm not even sure he did it on purpose although he claims he did. You've got to understand that Alvin is weird. He's even weirder than the other boys I know.

That afternoon I was supposed to be weeding a flower garden for Mom. I tried. I really did, but it was hot. Pretty soon those stupid marigolds started to look like scoops of ice cream to me. I have a big imagination when it comes to ice cream.

Now my grandpa owns Duncan's Drug Store and he serves the best ice cream around. He's always glad to see me and is usually good for a free cone. You know how grandpas are. I knew Mom wouldn't like it if she found out I was bothering Gramps again. However, Mom was watching her favorite soap, "As Our Lives Change." I washed my hands in the bird bath and made my escape.

When I got to the drug store, Gramps was cleaning the soda fountain. He had the sundae toppings down in front of him and the tops off of some of them.

Unfortunately, I was not Gramps' only customer. Alvin was there, too. I could see that he'd bought one of those dill pickles on a stick. Yuk. Why would anyone eat one? Of course Alvin is a jerk, so it figures.

I tried not to look at Alvin and I sat as far away from him as I could. Gramps would have to notice me sooner or later.

Alvin hadn't taken a bite of his pickle yet. Maybe it was too green and slimy even for him. He was just staring at Gramps.

At last Gramps noticed me and smiled. He wiped his hands on his apron and started over. I got all ready to tell him that I wanted bubble gum ice cream on the bottom and pistachio on the top.

Then, just as I got my mouth open, Alvin said in a really loud voice, "Aw heck!"

Gramps and I gave him our full attention. We know Alvin and we were expecting the worst.

"What's the matter?" Gramps asked nervously.

"I lost it," Alvin grumbled.

"Lost what?"

"My pickle."

"Your pickle," Gramps snorted. "Where did you lose it?"

"I dropped it in your stuff," Alvin answered.

"What stuff?" Gramps asked.

"In there," said Alvin. And he put his hand right in the hot fudge machine.

"Alvin!" Gramps screamed. "Stop! You'll burn your hand! You'll ruin the hot fudge!"

But by now Alvin was pulling a goopy mess out of the machine. It was dripping all over Gramps' clean counter. "Say, this might not be too bad," Alvin said thoughtfully.

"Your mother is going to hear about this," Gramps yelled as he started for Alvin.

"Yeah, not bad at all," Alvin slobbered. "I think I've invented something here."

"What you've invented is the biggest chocolaty mess in history. And if you don't take that thing outside, I'm going to throw you out," Gramps threatened.

About that time Alvin looked up and saw Gramps waving his fist. "Hey, don't get mad. I'm going. You ought to try one of these," he yelled as he raced for the door.

Gramps stopped at the door and leaned on the door frame for a minute. "That boy," he groaned. "I'm too old for the likes of him. What a mess!"

Poor Gramps had to wipe the fudge sauce off the floor and the counter. Then he had to wash his rag and change aprons. I tried to help, but he wouldn't let me.

"Bad enough to get me all sticky and cranky. Just stay out of the way," he grumbled.

Finally, Gramps was ready to make my cone. He asked me what I wanted and I told him about the bubble gum and pistachio. He frowned, but he picked up his ice cream scoop.

Just then three boys from my class came in. They were excited.

Joey Brown said, "We want one of those new fudge things."

"One of those things like Alvin has," Butch Ramey nodded.

Gramps turned around and looked at them. "You do?" he said doubtfully. "Do you know what's under all that fudge sauce?"

"Heck no," Joey shrugged. "But Alvin says it's good."

"He said he just invented it and we ought to try it," Butch added.

"Boys, that thing Alvin has is an accident," Gramps explained. "I don't think you really want one."

"Sure we do," Joey insisted.

"If Alvin's got one, we want one," Butch agreed.

Gramps sort of thought that over for a minute. Then I saw a little smile start at the corners of his mouth. "Okay," he said. "I guess it's time I let you in on our little secret."

Chapter 2

I figured Gramps would just take a couple of dill pickles out of his jar. He'd dunk them in the hot fudge sauce and the boys would change their minds.

Instead, Gramps got sneaky. "Those new things are in the back of the store," he explained. "They're still in the experimental stage so I can't let just anyone have one. They cost a dollar apiece, too. Have you got that much?"

The boys dug down in their pockets and pulled out everything but money at first. Finally on the counter, there were three dollars in pennies, nickles, dimes and quarters.

"Three green monsters coming up," Gramps said cheerfully as he disappeared.

"Did you hear that?" Butch said eagerly. "He called them Green Monsters. With a name like that, they've got to be good."

"Yeah. First he said they were an accident. Then he said they're in the experimental stage. We're really on to something," Joey agreed.

"That remains to be seen," Freddy Flint said solemnly.

Then Gramps was back. He had three small packages that looked like hot dogs. What an act he put on!

"Now boys," he said in a hushed voice. "I've been thinking about this. I don't want any spies from the other ice cream stores to find out about these. You've got to promise to eat them where no one will see you and not to tell anyone."

The boys looked at each other. They were impressed.

"Oh, sure," Joey said quickly. "We promise."

"You bet," Butch agreed.

"How about you?" Gramps asked Freddy.

"What if they make us sick?" Freddy grumbled.

"They won't make us sick," Joey scoffed. "Now hurry up and promise."

Freddy made a face and said, "All right. I promise."

When the boys were gone, Gramps looked at me and I looked at him. He sort of "tee heed," and I giggled. Then he began to laugh and I laughed. We laughed until we cried.

When we couldn't laugh any more, Gramps said, "I haven't had so much fun in years. That ought to teach those boys a lesson."

"You said it, Gramps," I giggled. "I'd like to see their faces about now."

"I only hope their parents don't get mad at me," Gramps chuckled.

"I don't think they will," I assured him. "A dill

pickle isn't going to hurt anyone."

I had finally gotten my cone and started out the door. Suddenly, I was almost knocked over by a mob of about twenty kids. Alvin was in the lead and he had a big grin on his face.

"These guys want to try Green Monsters, too," he said proudly. "Maybe I should get a patent or something."

"Now wait a minute," Gramps objected. "Fun is fun, but this is too much."

"Aw please, Mr. Duncan," one of the kids pleaded. "We know they're still in the experimental stage. We won't tell anyone about them. Please?"

Gramps stood there a minute looking confused. Then he motioned me to come behind the counter. "Here's five dollars," he whispered. "Run over to Abernathy's Grocery and get two jars of pickles right away. Bring them to the back door, and hurry."

I got to Abernathy's as fast as I could. In a few minutes I was at the back door with the pickles.

Alvin met me. "Good work," he gasped. "You wouldn't believe what it's like out front now. Mr. Duncan says to take this ten dollar bill and bring as many pickles as you can carry."

Chapter 3

The drug store had to close early that day because Gramps ran out of hot fudge sauce. You should have heard the groan from the line of kids outside.

When the store opened the next morning, the line was almost a block long. Kids were pushing and shoving to be first.

Luckily, Gramps had hired several new workers to help him, and Alvin was one of them. Alvin's job was to stand at the door and hand out numbers. Then nobody could cut in line once they got in.

Everything went smoothly until old Mrs. Wriggly wobbled up leaning on her cane. She doesn't believe in standing in line. Maybe that's because she's the mayor's mother.

"Hey Sonny, what's going on here?" she demanded. "Some kind of a sale?"

"No, it's not a sale," Alvin explained. "We're

serving Green Monsters today. All these people are waiting to buy one."

"Green Monsters?" she fumed. "I say there are plenty of little monsters out here. Stand aside. I've got to get in and buy my stomach pills."

"Sorry," said Alvin. "You'll have to wait your turn. There isn't any room for you to get back to the pills right now."

"No room?" she said doubtfully. "What the heck is a Green Monster anyway? I've never heard of one."

"I'm glad you asked," Alvin said proudly. "They are a hot fudge treat that I invented yesterday. Mr. Duncan makes them for me."

"New, eh?" she cackled. "I believe I'll try one. Got to keep up with the kids, you know."

"Fine, fine," said Alvin. "But you'll have to wait your turn."

Mrs. Wriggly glared at Alvin. "Young man," she said angrily, "I've done business with George Duncan for over forty years. Don't tell me that I've got to wait in line just to . . ."

By now Gramps had heard the commotion and he came rushing out. "Let this lady in, Alvin," he ordered. "She has to have her medicine."

"I don't want medicine," she informed him. "I want one of those Green Monsters. This fellow tells me I have to wait in line."

"Oh, no, Mrs. Wriggly," Gramps said soothingly. "Come right in. Let me get you some of your medicine now and . . ."

"I said I want a Green Monster and that's what I'm going to get," she insisted as they disappeared.

A little while later Mrs. Wriggly came out chuckling.

"The latest thing. Still in the experimental stage and I've got one," she bubbled. Gramps just stood at the door shaking his head.

Two men drove up in their garbage truck about 10:30. "Hey Alvin," the driver called. "What's the line for?"

"We're serving something new," Alvin called back. "They're called Green Monsters."

"We stop here every morning at this time for coffee and donuts. We haven't got time to wait in line," the man grumbled.

By now Gramps had his eye on Alvin. "Hello, men," he called from the door. "Should I bring you coffee and donuts 'to go'?"

18

"Hmmm," the man considered. "What's this new Green Monster thing? Maybe we should have some of them instead."

"Oh, I doubt you would like them," Gramps explained. "They're just something Alvin invented for the kids. It's a green middle with hot fudge sauce all over it."

"Sounds interesting," said the man. "Bring us two of those instead of the coffee and donuts."

"All right," Gramps sighed.

Before long Mrs. Scott came along. At first she was sneezing so hard that she didn't notice the line. As she bumped into one of the kids, she sniffled, "How come there's a line at the drug store? I've got to get some cough drops and tissues."

Alvin shrugged. "I'd like to let you in, but there isn't any room inside. You'll have to wait your turn."

"I belong in bed," Mrs. Scott coughed. "You've got to let me in."

Again Gramps appeared in the nick of time. "Why Mrs. Scott, you look terrible," he said kindly. "I know what you need."

"What do you mean 'I look terrible'?" she objected. "I came here for cough drops and tissues. How dare you tell me how bad I look!"

"I only meant that I can see you have a cold,"

Gramps said quickly. "Come right in and we'll have you on your way home again in a jiffy."

When Mrs. Scott reappeared she did have a box of tissues under one arm. She had a little bag, too, that probably held the cough drops. However, she also had a Green Monster and a smile on her face.

Just then a big Cadillac drove up. "It's the mayor," somebody said.

"Oh, no," groaned Gramps. "I'll bet he's here to talk to me about his mother. What am I going to tell him?"

Chapter 4

Although the mayor's office is only a block from the drug store, Mayor Wriggly drives everywhere. I suppose that car makes him feel important. Or maybe he gets a kick out of parking in No Parking zones.

Gramps greeted him with a sickly smile. "Mayor, if it's about your mother," he began.

"Well yes, I am here because of my mother," the mayor nodded.

"I tried to get her to take some stomach pills and forget about Green Monsters," Gramps explained. "She absolutely insisted on trying those new things."

The mayor laughed. "That's Mom. She always has to have her way. Anyway, I'm delighted that she bought one of those new things."

"You are?" gasped Gramps. "Why with her stomach problems, I thought that she would have . . ."

"Her stomach is fine," snorted the mayor. "She just takes those pills to have something to do. Now tell me about these monsters."

Gramps sighed. "To be honest, Mayor, they started out because of an accident that Alvin had. We never expected them to be such a big hit."

"So what?" said Mayor Wriggly. "Some of the world's greatest inventions started out as accidents. The important thing is that people buy them."

"But, but," started Gramps.

"But nothing, George," the mayor interrupted. "I think you and Alvin have something here. My lawyer is on his way over. Let's go somewhere and talk a little business. Have Alvin come, too."

A skinny, young man with an attaché case hurried up almost at once. "Sorry to be so slow, sir," he said worriedly. "I couldn't find a parking place." Then he noticed the line. "What are all these people doing here? Are you selling out or something, Duncan?"

"No, no, nothing like that," the mayor assured him. "George and Alvin have invented something big. I've asked you to come because I want to make them a business offer."

"Oh," cooed the lawyer. "In that case, where can we talk?"

Everyone was looking at Gramps so he said,

"Well, I guess we could go in the pill department. That's pretty quiet today."

"Can Kristy take care of my job?" Alvin wondered.

Gramps nodded and suddenly I was part of things.

The four of them were gone for a long time. When they came out, the mayor and Alvin were grinning. Gramps looked as if he'd gotten a headache in the pill department.

"Now that we've got a deal," the mayor winked, "we need publicity. I'll send over a reporter from the paper right away."

"But, but . . ." Gramps began.

"Come on, George," the mayor stopped him. "Think positive. Green Monsters are going to put Littletown on the map."

"He's right, Mr. Duncan," said Alvin. "This is going to be the start of big things."

Miss Bliss, the reporter, was a chubby little woman who carried a huge camera. She seemed eager to get the photos first. The story would come later.

The mayor had Alvin bring him a Green Monster. The first twenty-five pictures were of him eating it. Then, Alvin had to bring lots of napkins. The mayor wanted people to remember his face without hot fudge at election time.

At last it was time for pictures of Alvin and Gramps. The mayor suggested they stand with their arms around each other and look pleased. I thought it looked sort of dumb, but no one asked me. Finally, Miss Bliss put the camera in her car and they all went inside for the interview.

When they came out again, the mayor had his arm around Alvin. "Yes siree, boy. I like the way you think," he grinned. "A whole chain of places selling Green Monsters. Why Littletown will be famous. All that money will be coming here to roost."

Miss Bliss was smiling, too. "This really is a big story," she bubbled. "One of the city papers might even run it."

However, Gramps didn't look very happy. When the mayor and Miss Bliss had gone, he asked Alvin a question. "Whatever made you say all that stuff about starting a chain?"

Alvin shrugged. "Well, I did say 'maybe.'"

Chapter 5

The next day there was a big photograph of Mayor Wriggly in the paper. He was eating one of the fudge pickles. The caption said "MAYOR MEETS MONSTER." According to the story, Jones and Duncan would be issuing stock in a new corporation soon. It also said that they planned to build "Monster Palaces" all over the state.

As soon as I saw Gramps, I asked him about the story. "Are you really going to start a corporation? Will there really be things called 'Monster Palaces' everywhere?"

Gramps gave me a miserable look. "How do I know?" he shrugged. "This thing we've created really is a monster. Heaven only knows where it will all end."

The mayor was at the drug store a lot after that. He worried if there was no line outside. One day he offered free monsters to anyone living twenty miles away. When the radio announced that, the store was mobbed. The next day only people from fifty miles away could get one. We gave away hundreds. Soon the mayor was renting billboards all over the state. He hired airplanes to tow ads across the sky.

Then one morning he came into the store really excited. "Wait until you hear my latest idea," he told us. "This is the biggest of all. We're going to send the President a Green Monster."

"Oh, boy. That's a great idea," Alvin cheered.

"The President?" Gramps objected. "How are you going to keep the thing from getting cold before he gets it? Those things are bad enough hot."

"I've got that all figured out," the mayor explained eagerly. "The President will be in Cincinnati in a few days. We'll have a special hot foods truck deliver it. I know he'll be curious and open it right away. Think of the publicity—radio, TV, national newspapers."

"What if he takes a bite and hates the thing?" worried Gramps.

"He wouldn't dare admit it," Mayor Wriggly laughed. "The plan is perfect."

"I like it, I like it," yelled Alvin as he jumped up and down. "Let's rent a hot foods truck and deliver it ourselves."

"Hmmm," said the mayor, thinking it over.

"Well, I'm not going to Cincinnati," Gramps said firmly. "Somebody's got to mind the store."

"Fine, fine," the mayor agreed. "Alvin and I can handle this."

So the mayor borrowed a lunch wagon from one of his cousins. The pickle could be in its refrigerator and the hot fudge warm on its stove until the last minute.

Alvin found a big box that he painted green. He punched air holes in the sides and printed "Caution: Monster" on the top.

I wondered if the President would even dare to open it.

Miss Bliss took pictures of the mayor and Alvin as they left town. The mayor wore a big smile.

"We'll bring the President greetings from Littletown," the mayor proudly announced. "Be sure to print that."

"Don't tell him where you're from until he tastes the thing," Gramps yelled.

Two days later when the lunch wagon returned, the mayor looked miserable.

"What happened? What did the President say?" Gramps worried.

"He didn't say anything," mumbled Mayor Wriggly.

"We never got close to the President," Alvin moaned.

"We had to give the Green Monster to one of the Secret Service men," the mayor explained.

"That guy will probably eat it and the President will never see it," Alvin said gloomily.

Gramps didn't seem at all disappointed. "Oh, well," he said. "It was a nice try anyway. Better luck next time."

The next day Gramps was at the barber shop while Alvin and I helped out at the drug store. Suddenly Alvin hissed, "Look at those two guys!"

Sure enough there were two nasty-looking guys in trench coats leaning on the counter of the soda fountain.

"I see what you mean," I whispered. "Trench coats, and it isn't even raining."

"Maybe they're spies or the Mafia," Alvin whispered back.

The lady behind the counter was pointing at us now and the men were coming our way. It was too late to hide.

"We're looking for George Duncan and Alvin Jones," one man growled. "The President sent us."

"Uh, what did you want to see them about?" Alvin gulped.

"That's for them to know," the other man barked.

"Mr. Duncan is at the barber shop," Alvin said quickly. "I'll get him for you." And he bolted for the door.

"I'll help him," I said, racing after him.

We were panting so hard when we reached the barber shop that we could hardly talk.

"Slow down," said Gramps. "Now try that again. Who is it that wants to see me?"

"Gramps, those men said that the President sent them," I gasped.

"And they look mean," Alvin added.

Gramps sucked in his breath. "Oh, no," he groaned. "I knew we'd get into trouble with Mayor Wriggly's ideas!"

Chapter 6

The President's men were still at the drug store when we got back. However, they were eating vanilla ice cream cones. They didn't look quite as mean, now.

Gramps tried to smile and said, "I hear you gentlemen wish to see me. I am George Duncan."

"Well, well, well," the taller man said. "So you're the one who sent a monster to the President. Very funny."

"Yes, I guess I did," Gramps admitted. "It wasn't my idea, but I guess I am to blame."

"You ever tasted one of those things?" the man snorted.

Gramps shook his head.

"How about you kids?"

I shook my head. But Alvin said, "Sure, I'm the one that invented them."

"Aha," the tall man said triumphantly. "So you're Alvin Jones. You're the other one we're looking for."

Alvin gulped and nodded.

"Good," the man nodded. "You and your monsters have a problem."

Just then Mayor Wriggly charged through the door. "Welcome to Littletown," he boomed. "And how did the President like our little treat?"

"That's what we're here to talk about," the tall man said grimly. "Who are you?"

"Why I'm the mayor of this fair city," the mayor said, a little less eagerly. "I'm interested in the Green Monster's success."

"I see," the man frowned. "Then you can join us in our little talk. We need a quiet place for that."

"How about my office?" the mayor suggested.

"Sounds good. Let's go," the tall man agreed.

I went along, too. I figured that Gramps might need help.

When we got to the mayor's office the tall man handed Gramps his card. "Alfred Drake here. Secret Service," he explained.

Then he opened his attaché case and took out some papers. "I want you to read these," he ordered.

Gramps took the papers in shaky hands and the mayor read over his shoulder. When they got to the

fourth page, Gramps laid the papers down. "I give up," he pleaded. "I can't understand a word of this."

"I know what you mean," Drake shrugged. "Well, let me explain it to you. The President wants to know what's in those things of yours. So does the Food and

35

Drug Administration. Your Green Monsters have to have a package with a label listing ingredients."

Gramps let out a big sigh. "Of course," he agreed. "We'll take care of it right away."

"Not so fast," the mayor protested. "If people knew what they were really eating, they might not buy our product."

"So what do you think the law is for?" Drake said coldly.

"You don't understand," the mayor explained. "There's nothing dangerous in the Green Monsters. It's just that a dill pickle dunked in hot fudge sauce doesn't sound very tasty."

The Secret Service men made faces. "It sure doesn't," agreed the tall man. "You mean, people actually eat that?"

The mayor nodded. "You bet. We've had a line outside Duncan's Drug Store almost every day for a long time now. No complaints either."

Drake whistled. "Sounds like a real money-maker. No wonder you aren't wild about printing the ingredients. Still, the law is the law."

Everyone thought hard for a few minutes. Then Alvin said, "You know, I think the answer is right here in this paper from the government."

Gramps looked puzzled. "I can't understand a

word it says. How could it be the answer to anything?"

"That's just it," Alvin said brightly. "If we use big, fancy words to describe the pickle and the hot fudge, no one will understand."

The mayor grinned from ear to ear. "Good thinking, Alvin," he said. Then he gave Alvin a pat on the back.

"The boy has something there," Drake agreed.

* * * * * *

Mayor Wriggly searched for days to find just the right words to describe the Green Monster. He knew that a pickle is actually a cucumber that has been processed. The encyclopedia told him that the Latin name for a cucumber is *cucumis sativus*. The stuff listed on the hot fudge cans was already confusing. So, we had our list of ingredients. The government was satisfied and our customers never did find out what they were eating.

With one crisis out of the way, the mayor had another idea for promoting Green Monsters. He decided to have a special celebration in Littletown. It would honor Alvin as the inventor of "the monster." This was the start of another huge publicity campaign.

Chapter 7

A big parade was planned for Alvin Jones Day. One of the older girls in town was crowned "Miss Green Monster." The local fire department sold bumper stickers that said "Littletown—Home of Green Monsters." The ladies club planned a big picnic dinner. The town put up pictures of Green Monsters everywhere.

Alvin got to ride at the front of the parade with the mayor in his convertible. Gramps and I rode in a smaller car right behind them. I thought it was all pretty neat, but Gramps was embarrassed.

"You'd think I'd done something important," he mumbled.

I waved at the people as we went by and they waved back. They cheered and clapped for us, too.

The cars stopped in front of Gramps' store. A big platform covered with green paper was set up. We got to watch the rest of the parade from there. When the last marching band arrived, it was time for the speeches. The mayor went first.

"My fellow citizens of Littletown," he said into the microphone. "A wonderful thing has happened to us. Because of a new hot fudge treat invented right here, the nation will soon beat a path to our door. We have Alvin Jones to thank for giving us the Green Monster. This young genius came up with the secret recipe and shared it with the town. Now the fame of that invention has spread to our neighboring towns. We feel that Green Monsters will soon take over the country. Therefore, Alvin Jones, we are here to honor you. I would like to present you with the key to the city. Littletown is proud of you."

The people cheered and flashbulbs flashed as Alvin took the big cardboard key from the mayor. Then he stepped to the microphone.

"Ladies and gentlemen," Alvin said. "I thank you one and all for this honor. I feel very lucky to have invented something so popular. I'd like to thank Mr. Duncan for his help and Mayor Wriggly for all his encouragement."

As Alvin sat back down, the crowd went wild. He had to stand up again and take a bow.

Then the mayor looked at Gramps. Into the microphone he said, "And now I'd like to have George Duncan say a few words about his part in all of this. George . . ."

Gramps looked up and shook his head, but the mayor insisted. At last Gramps walked slowly to the microphone. He cleared his throat several times and wiped his glasses.

Finally he said, "I do want to thank you all for being so nice. Littletown is a great place to live, and I think it's time you knew the truth about the Green Monster."

The crowd got very quiet and Mayor Wriggly hurried over. Snatching the mike from Gramps, the mayor said, "Uh, thank you, George. I know you're dying to remind everyone how truly good your product is. But we're almost ready for the big "Monster Feed." In a minute there will be half-priced treats for everyone. Right now I'd like to have Alvin Jones serve me the first Green Monster of our celebration."

The crowd smiled and clapped as Alvin took a tray from someone at the edge of the platform. He was walking toward the mayor with the silver wrapped package when suddenly he tripped. The tray went flying and the "monster" landed in the coils of microphone cord.

Frantically, Alvin grabbed at the little silver package. He did manage to get hold of the "monster's" stick. Unfortunately, all of its wrapping and chocolate came off.

As he handed the thing to the mayor, Alvin said crossly, "Oh heck, there's nothing left but the pickle."

The microphone was on and everyone heard Alvin. The crowd began to mutter. "Pickle? The boy said 'pickle!' Is that what we've been eating?"

They sounded so angry that Gramps, Alvin, the mayor, and I ran into the drug store. We dashed past the vats of hot fudge sauce and slipped past a table of dill pickles. There wasn't time to reach the back door so we all hid behind the counter in the pill department.

The crowd was right behind us. "We'll find you, you crooks. Come out and face the music," they yelled. I was scared.

Then little by little the noise died down. I heard someone laugh. There was more laughing and the people were talking softly to each other.

Those of us hiding behind the pill counter looked at each other. We were puzzled. What was going on? We peeked over the counter and we couldn't believe what we saw.

People were standing around the hot fudge vats dipping all sorts of food. One lady was nibbling chocolate-covered grapes. A little girl was dipping French fries. Others had donuts and mushrooms, bread and tomatoes. They were having a great time.

"We're having a party. Care to join us?" a man offered.

It looked like so much fun that we agreed. Gramps grabbed a banana and the mayor took a cookie. Someone handed Alvin a piece of zucchini and I found some pretzels. We sampled each other's food and tried to decide which was best. For once, the whole town took time to visit.

Then gradually, everyone began to get full. At last even Alvin said, "I can't eat another bite."

"Me neither," Gramps groaned.

Old Mrs. Wriggly said, "This is such fun that I hate to see it end."

"I think I like hot fudge pickles after all," said the mayor's lawyer.

I said, "I think we ought to do this again."

The mayor looked thoughtful. "Well, maybe we should," he agreed. "Let's make it an annual event with a parade and the whole works."

"Will that put Littletown on the map?" Alvin asked with a grin.

"Yes, my boy, I think it just might," the mayor smiled.